For Mackenzie, who fills my
heart with happy notes
—RGG

To all Creatives, follow your passion,
chase your dreams, and never give up
—JRS

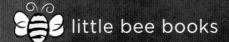 little bee books

New York, NY
Text copyright © 2021 by Rhonda Gowler Greene
Illustrations copyright © 2021 by James Rey Sanchez
All rights reserved, including the right of reproduction in whole or in part in any form.
Manufactured in China RRD 0521
First Edition
10 9 8 7 6 5 4 3 2 1
Library of Congress Cataloging-in-Publication Data is available upon request.
ISBN 978-1-4998-1172-8
littlebeebooks.com
For information about special discounts on bulk purchases,
please contact Little Bee Books at sales@littlebeebooks.com.

THIS MAGICAL, MUSICAL NIGHT

Words by Rhonda Gowler Greene
Pictures by James Rey Sanchez

little bee books

While notes are dreaming on the page,
musicians whisk onto the stage.

This concert hall? Filled to the brim!
The clock strikes eight. The lights go dim.

Oboe chirps her *A* and soon
the orchestra begins to tune.

Conductor enters from the wing.
Applause! A pause.
Then, instruments as one . . .

...all

Notes ascend—swoop and chase!

They curl, unfurl, swirl round this place!

Like a choir blending fine,

a *symphony!* So divine!

double basses—brawny fellows!

Swerving in their rounded rows,

a whisper-glide of graceful bows.

Add harp's angelic

pling . . . plung . . . plings!

And, *voilà!* Look!

We have the strings!

Who bursts in with velvet tones?

The brass! What class! Oh, bright trombones,

French horns, trumpets, tubas blow

with lips *abuzzzz* and great gusto!

Listen to those brilliant players

building lush harmonic layers.

Notes go soaring like an eagle.

How majestic! Royal. Regal.

Floating on a reedy breeze,

easing in with clicking keys—

the woodwinds! Clarinets and flutes!

Hear those highest lootle-oots!?

That's piccolo!
Her sweet birdcall.
The wee-est woodwind
of them all.

Notes now melt into a solo.

Eyes and ears are all on

oboe.

Then—

English horn? His bud, bassoon?

That clever duo makes us swoon!

Their nimble notes rise in crescendo,

soften to diminuendo. . . .

What's this?! A *tumble*, *bumble*, **BOOM!**

A *rrrrumbling* that shakes the room!

Percussion's mighty timpani!

The thunder of the symphony!

Then cymbals' lightning splash of—*CRASH!*

And xylophone's loud *plip-plop* dash!

The storm clears.

And light appears.

Ah, piano's blissful skills.

'Cross ivory, *arpeggio* spills.

Hear those thrilling frills of trills?

Whooosh! Glissando gives us chills!

The *tempo* slows, now more subdued.
How unique, each movement's mood.
It's like a magic music potion—
sounds excite, stir up emotion.

Puckish, prankish, lively, cheerful.

Spooky, melancholy, tearful.

Music! *Music!* Oh, how grand!

A language we all understand.

Allegro now, and we're in luck.
The strings—they're plucking!
Plick! Plick! Pluck!

Playful, perky *pizzicato*.
Bouncing bows,
then quick *spiccato!*

These musicians, all so gifted,
make our souls much lighter. Lifted.
This night is golden, like a treasure.
But now—too soon!—the final measure.

BUM!

bum

. . . bum bum bum BUMMMMMMmmmmmmmmmm!

A pause. Applause!

Bravissimo! A wild ovation

to convey our admiration!

BRAVO!

Musicians bow, whisk off the stage

while notes all dream upon the page.

ENCORE!

The music ends. But hearts are bright

from this magical . . .

. . . musical night.

Many classical music terms are Italian.
Italy has been an important center
for music for hundreds of years.

Allegro
fast and lively

Arpeggio
a broken chord
played in ascending
or descending
succession

Crescendo
a gradual increase
in volume

Diminuendo
a gradual decrease
in volume

Glissando
sliding one or more
fingers rapidly over
the keys of a piano or
strings of a harp

Pizzicato
plucking the strings
of an instrument with
fingers instead of
using a bow

Spiccato
lightly bouncing the
bow on a stringed
instrument

Tempo
the speed at which
a passage of music
is played